a minedition book

published by Penguin Young Readers Group

Published simultaneously in Canada.
Manufactured in Hong Kong by Wide World Ltd.
Typesetting in Veljovic, designed by Jovica Veljovic.
Color separation by Fotoreproduzioni Grafiche, Italy.

Library of Congress Cataloging-in-Publication
Data available upon request.

ISBN 0-698-40027-5
10 9 8 7 6 5 4 3 2 1
First Impression

For more information
please visit our website:
www.minedition.com

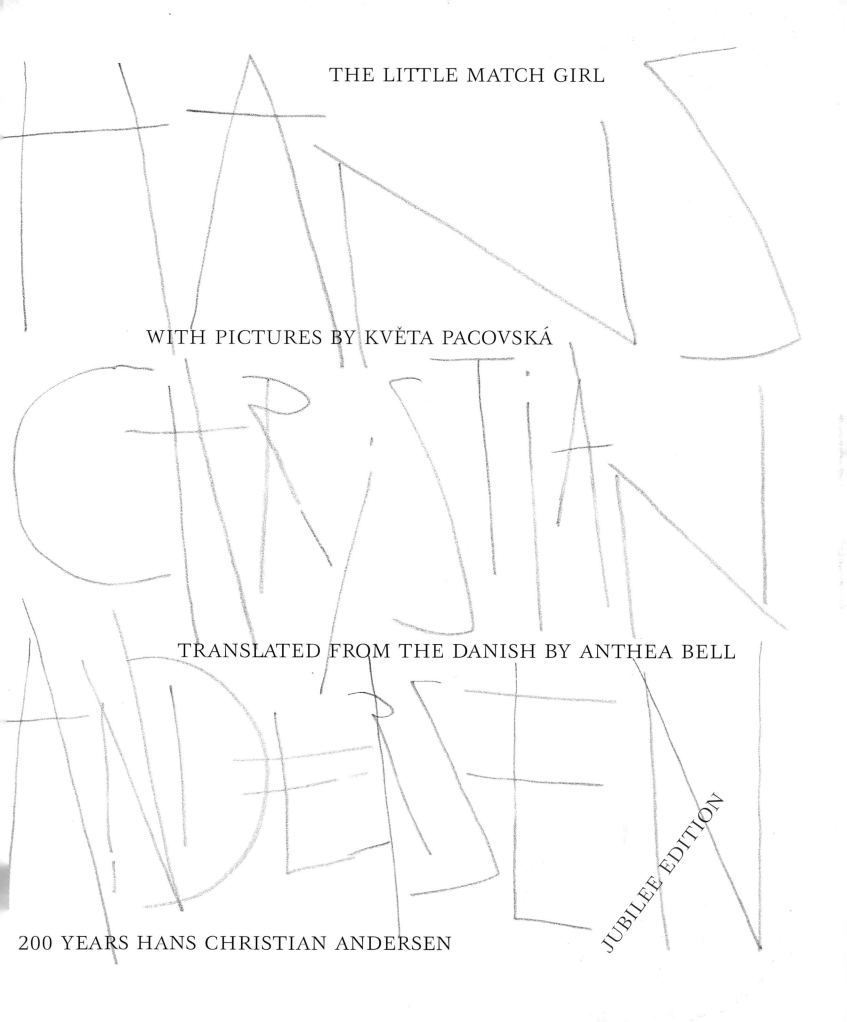

THE LITTLE MATCH GIRL

WITH PICTURES BY KVĔTA PACOVSKÁ

TRANSLATED FROM THE DANISH BY ANTHEA BELL

JUBILEE EDITION

200 YEARS HANS CHRISTIAN ANDERSEN

t was bitterly cold outside. Snow was falling, and the evening was beginning to grow dark, for this was the very last night of the year: New Year's Eve. A poor little girl came walking down the street in the cold and the dark, with her head and her feet bare. She had been wearing slippers when she left home, but they were no use, because they were much too big for her. Her mother had been the last to wear them, and they were so large that they came off the little girl's feet as she scurried over the road to avoid two carriages driving rapidly by. She had lost one slipper entirely, and a boy ran off with the other, shouting that he'd use it as a cradle when he had a baby of his own.

So now the little girl was walking along barefoot, and her feet were red and blue with the cold. She had matches for sale, carried in her old apron, and she was holding some of them out in a bundle, but no one had bought any matches from her all day long or given her even the smallest of coins.

The poor little thing was chilled to the bone and hungry, and she looked wretched. Snowflakes fell on the long yellow hair that curled so prettily behind her neck, but she never gave that a thought. Lights were shining in all the windows, and there was a delicious smell of roast goose in the streets because it was New Year's Eve. She couldn't stop thinking about that.

She sat down on the ground in a corner between two houses, one of them set a little farther back from the street than the other, and folded her little legs under her, trying to keep warm, but she only felt even colder. She dared not go home because she hadn't sold any matches or made any money at all, and her father would beat her. Anyway, it was cold at home too. They lived in an attic right under the roof, and the wind whistled through the holes in it. Straw or rags were stuffed into the biggest cracks to stop them up.

Her little hands were almost numb with cold. Oh, a match would do her good! If only she dared take one out of the bundle, strike it on the wall of the building, and warm her fingers! She took a match out and struck it – whoosh! How brightly it flared up!

The warm, clear flame was like a little light, and she cupped her hands around it. Then it seemed to the little girl that she was sitting in front of a big iron stove trimmed with shiny brass. The fire in the stove burned with a blissful warmth. The little girl stretched her legs out to get them warm too, but then the flame burned out, the big stove disappeared, and there she sat with only the spent match in her hand.

Data GIORNO/MESE ANNO	Causale	Data pagamento GIORNO/MESE ANNO	Onorari	Rimborsi	Contributo previdenziale	IVA	Totale	Imponibile IRPEF	Ritenuta d'acconto	Totale

Domicilio

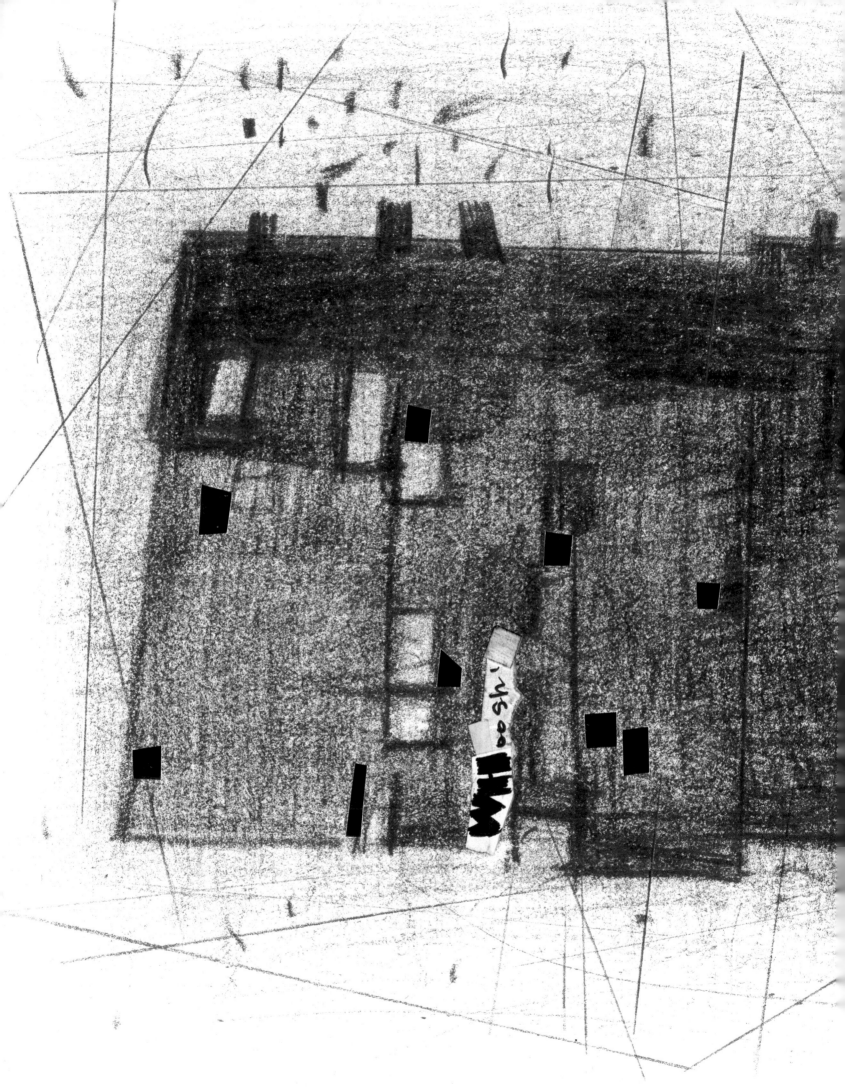

She struck another match. It too burned, shining brightly, and where the light fell on the wall it turned as transparent as gauze, and she could see right into the room inside. A table stood there, covered with a spotless white cloth and laid with fine china. On the table she saw a roast goose stuffed with prunes and apples, steaming hot and smelling delicious. More wonderful still, the goose jumped off its dish and waddled across the floor with a knife and fork in its back, as if it were coming straight over to the little girl. But then the match went out, and she saw nothing before her but the cold, solid wall.

She lit another match. Now she was sitting under a beautiful Christmas tree, even bigger and more prettily decorated than the one she had seen through the glass in the doors of the rich merchant's house at Christmas time. A thousand candles shone among its green branches, and pretty, bright pictures like the pictures in the windows of big stores were looking down at her. The little girl reached out both hands – but then the match went out, all the Christmas candles rose higher and higher in the air, and now she saw that they were the bright stars in the sky. One of them, a shooting star, fell and left a fiery trail behind it.

"Someone's dying!" said the little girl, for her old grandmother, the only person who had ever been kind to her, used to say that when you saw a shooting star it meant a human soul was going to God.

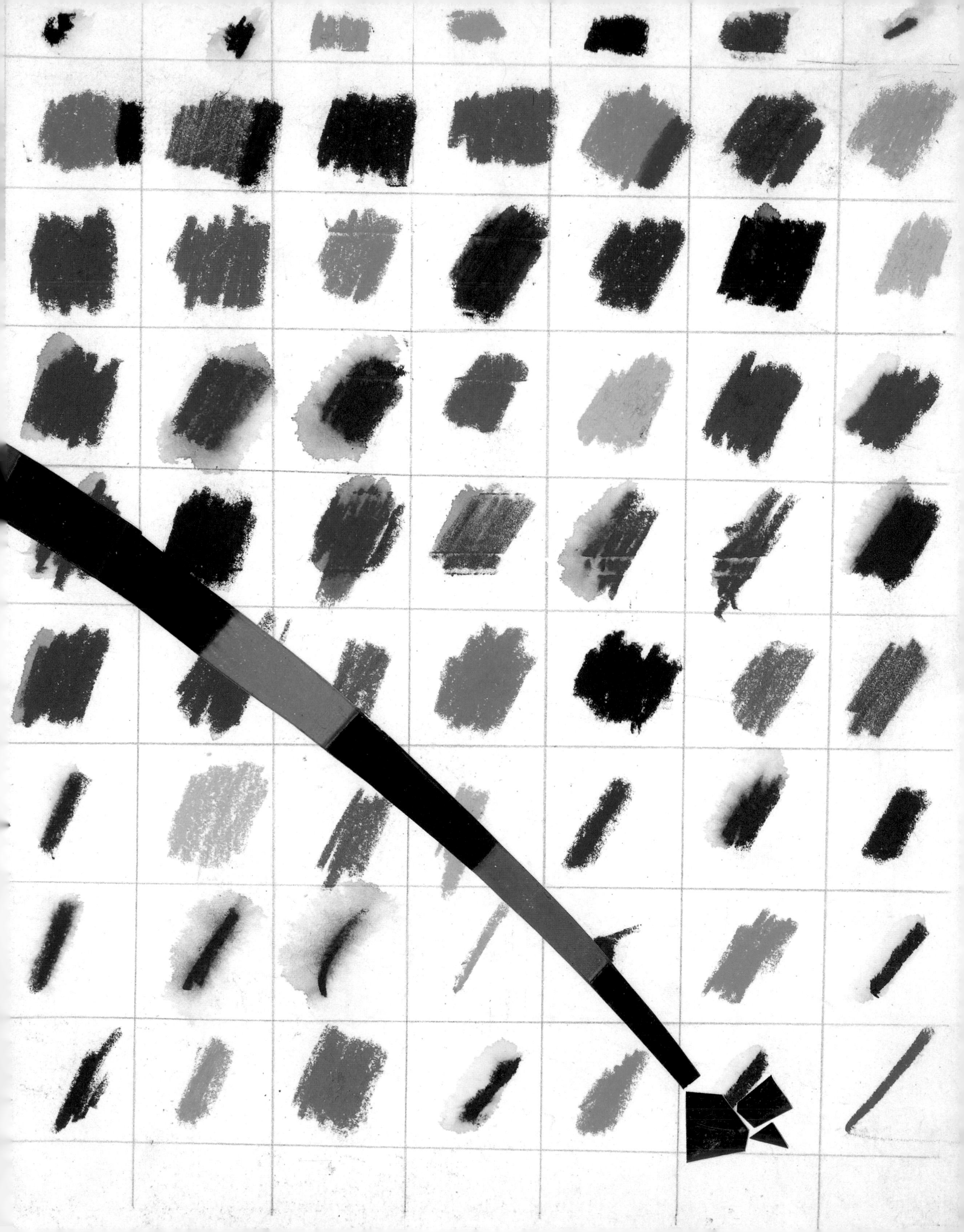

She struck another match on the wall. It cast a glow all around, and in that glorious light she saw her kind old grandmother, clear and shining bright. "Grandmother!" cried the little girl. "Oh, take me with you! I know that when the match goes out you'll vanish, like the warm stove, the delicious roast goose, and the lovely big Christmas tree."

Hoping to keep her grandmother with her, she quickly struck all the rest of the matches in the bundle. They shone with a flame that was brighter than daylight. Never before had Grandmother looked so tall and beautiful. She picked the little girl up in her arms, and they flew away in a halo of joy, up and up they soared, to a place where there was no more cold or hunger or fear, because they had gone to be with God.

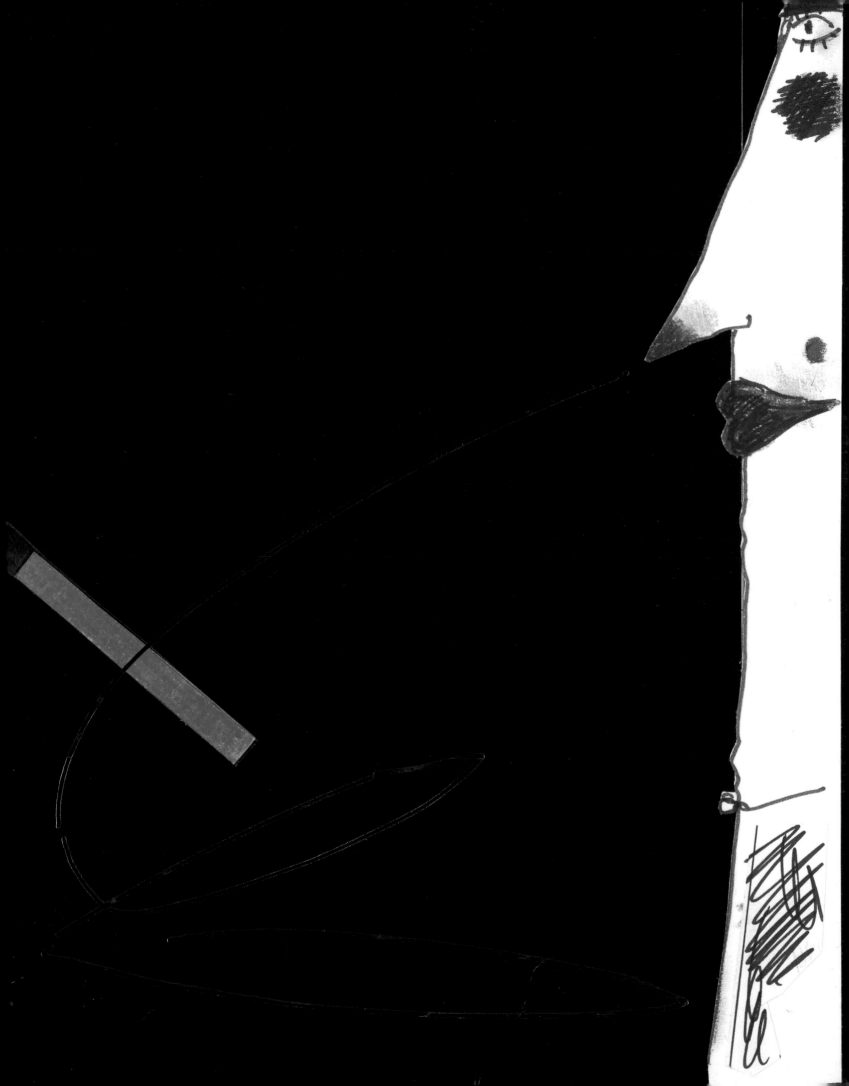

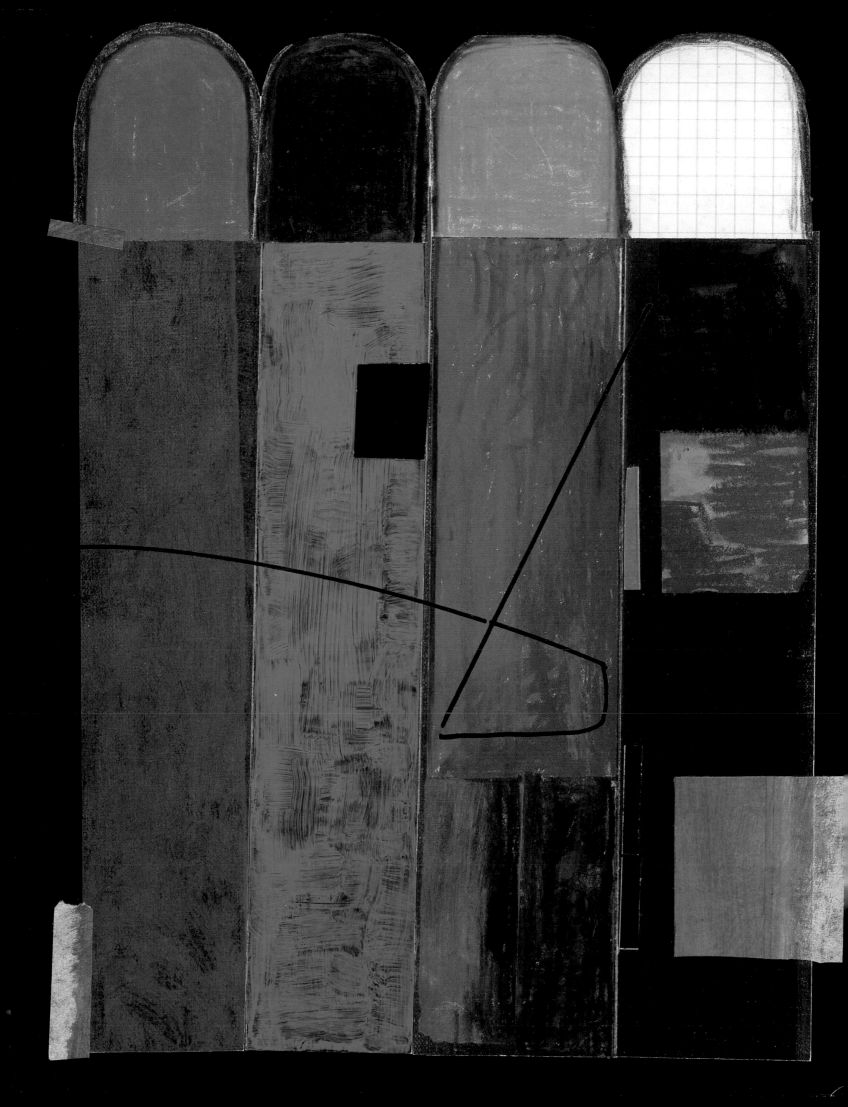

Next morning the little girl was found dead of cold, sitting in the corner between the two houses, her cheeks red and with a smile on her lips. She had frozen to death on the last night of the Old Year. New Year's Day dawned over her little body where she sat with the matches, almost all of them struck and spent. People thought she must have been trying to keep warm, but none of them knew what wonderful things she had seen, or how she had flown away in glory with her old grandmother into a Happy New Year.